# Emily

### and the

# Werewolf

# Emily
## and the
# Werewolf

by Herbie Brennan

illustrated by David Pace

LIBER PRESS

*to Jacks* HB

———

*for Charlotte* DP

# contents

## CHAPTER ONE

One morning on their way to school, Emily and her friends saw Farmer Osboro kicking a sheep. The animal was on the side of the road, cowering up against Mrs Roland's hedge, bleating pitifully as it tried to get away. It seemed to have escaped from Farmer Osboro's field.

The children stopped.

"I'll teach you!" Farmer Osboro was saying. "I'll teach you to waste my valuable time!" He was a large man, fat around the belly, and his colour, always high, was now positively purple. He aimed another kick.

"Excuse me," said Reggie McPhee, stepping forward.

Reggie was small but very brave. Emily thought she might quite like to marry him one day. He loved animals and had an interesting sister, who was also in the little party which had stopped.

Farmer Osboro spun round. "What?" he asked fiercely. "What? What?"

"Sir," said Reggie stoutly, "I don't think what you're doing is very nice."

"Nice?" echoed Farmer Osboro, as if he had never heard the word before. "Did you say nice?"

"I said it wasn't very nice," said Reggie firmly. "Our teacher, Mrs Wilson, told us we should be kind to animals."

Farmer Osboro looked from the small boy to the sheep and back again. He seemed to be having trouble believing what he saw. Eventually he gasped in a sort of strangled voice, "This ... is my ... sheep!"

But Reggie was not to be diverted. "Sir, that doesn't matter. You have to be kind to animals, whoever owns them. Or whoever doesn't," he added as an afterthought.

Farmer Osboro was turning from purple to puce. Emily had never seen an adult go puce before, but she thought it must be a danger sign. "What's your name, boy?" asked Farmer Osboro loudly.

"Reggie McPhee," Reggie muttered. He looked down at his knobbly knees, obviously wondering if he had bitten off more than he could chew.

"Speak up!" roared Farmer Osboro.

"Reggie McPhee!!" Reggie screamed in terror.

"Don't you shout at me, boy!" shouted Farmer Osboro. "How dare you shout at me!"

"But, Farmer Osboro —"

"Quiet, boy. When I want your stupid opinion I'll ask for it!" He swung round and began to walk threateningly towards Reggie. As he did so, his features changed.

Emily watched fascinated. Hair began to sprout on Farmer Osboro's cheekbones and not grey hair either, but hair so dark brown it was almost black. His eyes started to narrow and lengthen, turning upwards at the ends. To Emily's astonishment, the whites turned amber and the pupils, formerly blue, took on a brownish, speckled hue. Fur was growing on his forehead.

"How dare you," shouted
Farmer Osboro, "how dare you
shout at me!"

His nose was flattening and turning black.

In three steps it was a snout, nostrils wide and bestial.
Then, with a small ripping sound, his entire mouth pushed
outwards. His lips narrowed and rolled back, revealing enormous,
vicious teeth.

"You need," snarled Farmer Osboro through his new, enormous,
vicious teeth, "to learn some —"

His ears began to push upwards, sharpening themselves to a
point. They grew long until they too were enormous, like the ears of
a dog.

" — MANNERS!" screamed Farmer Osboro. He reached towards
the paralysed Reggie McPhee and as he did so, his hands became
things of fur and claws, lengthening enormously. The button on his

jacket pinged off to lodge like an eye in the topiary rooster that Mrs Roland had cut into her hedge. His shirt ripped and a muscular, furry chest bulged through. His trousers ripped —

(Emily thought about looking away since she knew it was very rude to stare at what showed when someone ripped their trousers, especially when an adult ripped his trousers. She thought about it, but decided to keep looking anyway.)

— and out popped a pointed, furry bum, complete with tail. It was like nothing Emily had ever seen in her entire life. She felt her jaw drop and her eyes widen into saucers.

Farmer Osboro's long, taloned, brown-furred hands gripped Reggie's collar and began to shake him violently. Reggie's head woggled backwards and forwards like that of a rag doll.

"Manners!" screamed
Farmer Osboro again
as foam spread

over his new muzzle. "Manners, manners, manners!"

He lifted Reggie by the scruff of the neck and began to swing him round and round above his head, like the rotor of a helicopter. Reggie wailed and the wail rose and fell with each circuit. Faster and faster Reggie was whirled, until his trailing feet were a blur.

"Manners!" howled Farmer Osboro and let go. Reggie sailed directly over the hedge and landed in the rose-bed inside Mrs Roland's garden.

"Manners!" snapped Farmer Osboro. Then, without another word, he tucked his sheep bodily underneath one arm and stamped away, his furred tail dragging on the pavement.

# CHAPTER TWO

"Is Reggie all right?" Emily asked his sister Wilhelmena.

"I think so," Wilhelmena said.

They were standing by Mrs Roland's garden gate, watching Reggie trying to climb out of the rose-bed. The difficulty was the thorns which were holding tightly to his woollen cardigan.

"Has anybody ever thrown him over a hedge before?" Emily asked.

"He's never mentioned it," said Wilhelmena.

Reggie solved the problem by removing himself from the cardigan, then removing the cardigan from the thorns. They both looked in a bad way by the time he'd finished.

"Wasn't it peculiar the way Farmer Osboro changed," said Emily.

"Yes," Wilhelmena agreed. "One minute he was talking ever so quietly, the next he'd gone all red in the face and was shout —"

"I didn't mean then," Emily said. "I meant afterwards, when he started to grow hair."

"Hair?" Wilhelmena echoed.

"When his teeth got big and his ears went all pointy."

"Teeth?" Wilhelmena frowned. "Ears?"

"When his trousers burst and his bum poked out and he grew

a tail," Emily said, wide-eyed at the memory.

"He didn't grow a tail," Wilhelmena said. "He doesn't have pointy ears either." She hesitated. "And you're not allowed to say 'bum'."

"No, he doesn't usually," Emily told her patiently. "He doesn't have any of it usually. That's why it was so peculiar when he changed."

"Doesn't have any of what?" Wilhelmena asked.

"Fur and big teeth and a tail and things like that."

"He doesn't have them now," Wilhelmena said. "Look." She pointed.

Farmer Osboro was climbing onto his tractor, which was parked a little way along the village street. He looked tweedy as ever and the only hair about his person was the grey hair on his head.

Emily blinked. "He wasn't like that a minute ago."

"Yes he was," Wilhelmena said. "He's always been like that."

Emily said, "A minute ago he grew hair all over his face and his ears went pointy and his teeth got big and fierce..." she bared her own dainty teeth in demonstration, "... and his trousers split and he had a tail and —"

"You're very silly," said Wilhelmena stiffly. "All you can think about is making jokes, but I don't think it was very funny." She tossed her head for emphasis. "After all, it was my brother Farmer Osboro threw over the hedge."

"I wasn't —" Emily began. But it was too late. Wilhelmena was flouncing off in the direction of their school, her skirt swinging angrily from side to side. The others had already gone ahead.

Emily hurried after them. Wilhelmena liked to make a fuss, but all the same it was obvious she really hadn't noticed Farmer Osboro grow hairy. Which was strange, because Wilhelmena must have been looking at him at the time. Everybody must have been looking at him at the time.

In the school playground, Little Willie Craig went past trying to make a yo-yo go up and down.

"Excuse me, Little Willie," Emily said politely.

Little Willie peered at her suspiciously. He often walked to school with the girls, but didn't much like talking to them. "Yes?" he asked.

"When Farmer Osboro threw Reggie McPhee over the hedge, did you notice he grew fur and big teeth and pointy ears and a tail?"

"I thought he just fell in the flowerbed," said Little Willie.

"Not Reggie — Farmer Osboro!"

"Grew a tail and teeth and ears and stuff?"

"Yes. Did you notice?"

But Little Willie was shaking his head. "No, I didn't. Is that what he did? Grew a tail and stuff? Honest?"

Little Willie was as thick as a brick. Emily walked away while he was still goggling after her, asking stupid questions. He hadn't seen Farmer Osboro change either. Wilhelmena hadn't seen it, Little Willie hadn't seen it …

"Madelene!" called Emily, skipping after Madelene O'Mara who was walking briskly towards the entrance marked GIRLS.

"Hello, Emily," said Madelene. "Wasn't it awful what Farmer Osboro did to poor Reggie? Do you think he's allowed to do that?"

"He's an adult," Emily said a little breathlessly. "Adults are allowed to do anything." She fell into step beside Madelene.

"Are they allowed to kill you?" Madelene asked seriously.

Emily cast her eyes to heaven in exasperation. With more important things on her mind she asked, "Did you see him grow a tail?"

"Farmer Osboro?" Madelene looked at her in delighted amazement. "Did he grow a tail?" She began to look around her, as if searching for the tailed farmer.

"Did you see?" asked Emily urgently. "Did you see him grow a tail and teeth and fur and pointy ears?"

"No," Madelene said uncertainly. "Is this a quiz?"

Emily walked away from her as well. The thing was, Madelene wasn't as thick as a brick. She was actually rather clever. If she hadn't seen Farmer Osboro change either …. If she hadn't seen Farmer Osboro change either … what? He hadn't changed? But she'd seen him change!

With just enough time left before the bell rang for class, Emily left the school yard and backtracked down the village street to the exact spot where Farmer Osboro had kicked the sheep. She glanced around to make sure no-one was watching, then reached up and shook the rooster that Mrs Roland had cut into her hedge.

A button fell out. The button from Farmer Osboro's jacket. The button that had pinged off when he changed. There it was, on the pavement, proof positive she'd really seen what she thought she'd seen. Emily popped the button into the pocket of her dress and walked back towards the school, wondering what to do next.

## CHAPTER THREE

"Mummy ...?" Emily said uncertainly. Her mother, who was cooking dinner, looked tired. But then she nearly always did.

"Yes, darling?" her mother said absently.

"What do you call a man who grows fur and a tail and pointy ears and claws and big teeth and looks very scary?"

"Is this a joke, darling?" her mother asked cheerfully. "Like 'What do you call a squirrel who's carrying a sub-machine-gun?'"

"No, Mummy," Emily said seriously. "I just wanted to know."

"A man who grows fur and a tail and ...?" Her mother suddenly stopped frowning. "Oh, I know what you mean! That's a werewolf, darling. They don't exist."

Emily said, "If they don't exist, why have they got a name?"

"Well, they don't exist in real life, but people make films about them," her mother told her. "Teen Wolf, for instance. Michael J. Fox was in that. You like Michael J. Fox, don't you?"

"Yes," Emily said, although she didn't want to talk about Michael J. Fox just now. "I didn't see that movie."

"Well, he made it quite a long time ago. Before he was really famous. Actually nobody takes werewolf movies very seriously.

But people used to believe in them — werewolves, I mean."

"Why?" Emily asked.

"Why what, darling?" Her mother cut a potato in half and dropped both pieces into a pot.

"Why did people used to believe in them when they didn't exist?"

"Because people weren't very clever in those days," her mother said. "They believed in all sorts of things that didn't exist. They believed in sea serpents. They believed in dragons. They believed in fairies. None of these things existed, but people believed in them because they weren't very clever. They even believed the Earth was flat at one time."

Emily's mother believed something too. She believed a branch of Magnum Supermarkets was about to open in the village where they lived. She also believed that when the supermarket opened, she and

Emily would starve. Emily's mother had run the little village grocery shop since Emily's father died. She believed the new supermarket would take all her customers away.

"What would happen," Emily asked, "if in among all those silly things that people believed in — the dragons and the sea serpents and so on — what would happen if just one of them really did exist?"

"You mean like a dragon?"

"Or a werewolf." Emily nodded.

Her mother dropped the last potato into the pot and wiped her hands on a tea-towel. "Well, if it really existed, sooner or later somebody would see it. And since nobody has seen any of those nasty things people used to believe in, it proves they don't exist. Have you ever seen a dragon?"

"No," Emily said. She was thankful her mother hadn't asked if she'd ever seen a werewolf.

"There you are then," said her mother. "Will you pass me the carrots. We're going to have carrots tonight."

Emily slipped down off her chair and went to the larder where she found a plastic bag of pre-washed carrots. As she handed them to her mother, she said, "These werewolves that don't exist — what do they do?"

"In the movies, you mean?"

"I suppose so," Emily said. Then, on inspiration, "What did people used to believe they did?"

Emily's mother took three large carrots from the bag, hesitated, then took out another one. She lifted the knife she had used on the potatoes and began to scrape the carrots. "People believed —" Scrape, scrape. "— People believed a werewolf was a very peculiar sort of man who turned into a wolf every so often. When he got very hungry, or very angry."

"Every so often?" Emily echoed.

"I told you people weren't very clever in the old days."

"So every so often, anybody who was a werewolf grew fur and a tail and big teeth and ears?" Emily asked, taking care not to show how excited the whole conversation was making her feel.

"That's what they believed," her mother said with emphasis.

"And this happened —" Emily stopped to correct herself. "And they believed this happened when they got very angry."

"Yes."

"Then what happened?" Emily asked.

"Then they attacked people."

Emily took a deep breath. "You mean like throwing them over hedges?"

Emily's mother began to chop the carrots expertly into discs, which she dropped into a different saucepan from the potatoes. "Well, I've never heard of a werewolf throwing anybody over a hedge. Mostly they just, I suppose, ate people. Like a real wolf would."

Emily couldn't recall any teeth marks on Reggie, although it was just possible she might have missed them in the excitement.

"But they could throw people over hedges, couldn't they? If they wanted to?"

"I imagine they could," her mother said. "I imagine they could do anything."

So Farmer Osboro was a werewolf. He'd been very angry, so he'd grown fur and a tail and big teeth and claws and attacked Reggie McPhee. The trouble was, he'd go on attacking people every time he changed and he was going to change every time he got angry. What was she going to do?

"What did people do about werewolves?" Emily asked. As an afterthought she added, "When they still believed in them?"

"I'm sure I don't know," her mother said. She lit the gas and put both saucepans on to boil, then took out the grill pan and left it on the work top. She turned to the fridge to take out the pieces of haddock she and Emily were going to have for dinner. Emily hated haddock.

"Of course they didn't have to do anything about them," her mother went on, "since they didn't exist in the first place. They only believed they had to do something about them."

"What did they believe they had to do?" Emily persisted.

"I don't know," her mother said a little shortly. She was obviously getting fed up with werewolf questions.

Somebody had to know what to do about werewolves. But who? Emily suspected most people would be like her mother, not believing in them. Emily herself wouldn't have believed in them if she hadn't seen Farmer Osboro change before her very eyes. (And found the button in the hedge.) But she seemed to have been the only one to have seen him change. So she was probably the only person in the entire world who still believed in werewolves. She wished she could read better. There must be books that told you what to do about werewolves. Old books hidden away in dusty attics. Books written in the days when people still believed in them.

She wondered if she could find such a book and get her mother to read it to her. It seemed simple enough, but somehow she knew her mother was bound to ask her why she was so interested in werewolves. And if Emily admitted she'd watched Farmer Osboro change into one, her mother would conclude she was eccentric.

"Mummy ...?" Emily said.

Her mother laid the haddock pieces on the grill. "Yes, dear?"
"What **do** you call a squirrel who's carrying a sub-machine-gun?"
"'Sir'," her mother said and grinned.

# CHAPTER FOUR

Next day, which was Saturday, Emily discovered werewolves weren't the only of life's little problems. Since there was no school, as soon as she had helped her mother tidy up, Emily had the day to herself.

"What are you going to do today, Emily?" her mother asked just before she went off to open the shop. Saturday was a particularly busy day in the shop and by Saturday night, Emily's mother always looked even more exhausted than usual. Not that she ever complained, but between the long hours and the worry about the Magnum Supermarket, the strain was certainly beginning to tell.

"I thought I'd tidy up the house and then go for a little walk," said Emily. She tried to do as much as she could to help her mother about the house.

"That's very nice," her mother said with feeling. Impulsively she kissed Emily. "I don't know what I'd do without you now that Ralph..."

Ralph was Emily's father. Emily's mother had been about to say 'gone' or perhaps even 'dead' before she remembered she mustn't upset Emily. Emily, who knew her Daddy was in heaven, didn't really feel upset, but was careful not to tell her mother, who would have been upset that Emily wasn't upset.

"You have a nice day, Mummy," Emily said. She hoped her mother wasn't going to cry. She had enough problems with werewolves without having to worry about her mother crying.

"Thank you, dear." Her mother brushed away an errant tear but did not actually cry. "Don't go too far when you take your walk and don't forget to look both ways before you cross the road."

"I will, Mummy," Emily promised as her mother closed the door. They lived in a self-contained flat behind the shop, so she hadn't very far to go.

Emily began to tidy. Most of the mess was her own, but that didn't matter. She put things under things and straightened things and squared off things and fairly quickly their living room looked as if it hadn't been lived in for a while. She went to the cupboard and took out a bright red feather duster which she used to dust anything that wasn't likely to get broken. (Her mother, while she appreciated the help, didn't allow Emily to dust things that were likely to get broken.)

Then, with a feeling of real pride, she put away the duster and brought out the sweeping brush. She was small for her age so it was almost too big for her to use, but she began to push it across the kitchen floor, back and forth, back and forth.

After a moment, she seemed to be surrounded by a cocoon of concentration. She liked the feeling very much, because it helped her think. Part of her thought about Farmer Osboro turning into a werewolf, but another part, a bigger part, thought about her grandmother.

Every Sunday, Emily's mother and Emily visited Emily's father's mother, a widow who lived in a tiny, very warm thatched cottage at the south end of the village. Emily liked her grandmother and liked visiting her grandmother because the trees at the back of the cottage reminded her of Little Red Riding Hood. She often imagined herself walking through the trees to visit her grandmother and meeting up with the Wolf. It was sort of scary imagining a thing like that, but fun too. At least it had been fun before she met up with the real life wolf, Farmer Osboro.

Once, a long time ago, Emily had asked her grandmother if she minded living near the woods and risking being eaten by a wolf. Her grandmother told her seriously there weren't any wolves in the woods of England any more, but even if there were, she had The Maggot to protect her. The Maggot was her grandmother's tomcat, an enormous black and white beast who climbed on Emily's knee and placed forepaws around her neck and nuzzled her cheek with his great, broad, purring head. Emily could not imagine him protecting anyone.

The thing was, Emily thought, her grandmother was extremely old — several hundred years old at least — which meant she had been a young girl in the days when people believed in werewolves. And if she had lived in those days, she might remember what to do about them. She might, in short, have the solution to Emily's problems with Farmer Osboro.

But though she would visit her grandmother tomorrow, Emily knew she could not ask her grandmother about werewolves tomorrow. Emily's mother would be there and Emily's mother was already fed up with werewolves as a topic of conversation. Emily needed to see her grandmother alone.

Emily put the brush back in its cupboard and closed the door. She had already decided she would visit her grandmother today. Indeed, since she had finished tidying and cleaning, she would visit her grandmother now.

She wondered whether she ought toput on a coat in case of rain. There was a plastic hat in the pocket to protect against downpours, but since a glance through the window told her it was sunny outside, she decided against it. She left the flat the same way her mother had and walked through the shop to reach the village street. There were three customers waiting to be served, all ready to take their custom elsewhere once the new supermarket opened.

"Just off for my little walk, Mummy," Emily called innocently.

"All right, dear," her harassed mother called back. "Have a nice time."

It wasn't exactly a lie, Emily consoled herself. Grandmother's cottage wasn't very far away. All the same, she felt a little guilty not mentioning exactly where she was going.

The little garden at the front of her grandmother's cottage was full of scratching chickens. Several of them followed Emily to the front porch. She pushed open the half door and walked across the red-tiled hallway towards the little living room calling, "Hello Grandmother — it's Emily."  But there was no-one there.

"Grandmother!" Emily called as she walked through the house. No grandmother appeared.

Emily sat on a chair in the kitchen to think. She wasn't expected, so she shouldn't be surprised that her grandmother had gone out. But where? The most likely place was shopping, except that she always shopped at Emily's mother's shop, so Emily would certainly have passed her on the way. Besides, her cottage was left open and she always locked the door if she was going far. So she had to be somewhere close at hand.

Emily folded her hands on her lap and waited. After a while she got fed up with waiting and looked in her grandmother's cake tin. It was as empty as the cottage. She decided to see if her grandmother was out the back.

As she stepped through the back door, something brushed firmly against her leg. Emily looked down. "Hello, Maggot," she said.

"Wah," said The Maggot loudly. He polished her ankle.

"I don't suppose you know where Grandmother is?" asked Emily. She reached down to stroke his arching back.

"Wah," The Maggot said again. He walked purposefully along the narrow path. When Emily did not follow, he turned and looked at her. "Wah," he said again.

"Do you want me to follow you?" Emily asked.

It almost seemed as if The Maggot nodded. "Wah."

"All right," said Emily.

She walked round the side of the house and followed The Maggot along the narrow path that led past the hen-house to the old wooden barn marking the far edge of her grandmother's property. Emily had always been warned to keep away from the barn. Her grandmother said it was unsafe.

"I'm not allowed to go there, Maggot," Emily told The Maggot.

But he ignored her protest and sauntered on, his tail curled into a high-flying question mark. Emily followed him reluctantly. Perhaps her grandmother was in the barn and perhaps something had happened to her if the barn was unsafe.

The Maggot walked to the huge front doors of the barn, stretched and sharpened his claws. By the look of the wood, it wasn't the first time. He glanced round at Emily. "Wah," he said.

Nervously, Emily approached the doors and pushed. They were locked. "We can't get in," she told The Maggot.

The Maggot scratched the door again, more vigorously this time. He kept glancing at Emily.

"Is Grandmother in there?" Emily asked.

"Wah," said The Maggot.

Bravely, briskly, Emily knocked on the door. She waited. Nothing happened. She looked at The Maggot. "I don't believe she's in there," she said.

The Maggot tossed his head and sauntered off behind the barn. After a moment, Emily followed. There was a stack of old wooden crates beneath a dusty window. The Maggot leaped gracefully from one to the other until he was framed against the glass.

Emily hesitated again then, against all her better judgment, began to clamber up the crates. "I'm sure she really isn't in there," she told The Maggot as she reached the top. She looked through the window.

Her grandmother was inside all right. She was stirring a huge black cauldron which stood in the very centre of a wide chalk circle drawn on the floor of the barn. She was wearing a long black dress and a tall black pointed hat. Both were covered with embroidered stars and moons. Around her were heaps of dried herbs. Beside her was an old-fashioned broom, a polished wooden staff and something that looked suspiciously like a wand. Bats flew overhead. She was chanting something that sounded like *"Mano, spano, deeply pano! Kerplunk, kerplink und bookim, dano!"*

"Good grief!" Emily exclaimed so loudly that The Maggot backed off in alarm. "Grandmother is a witch!"

# CHAPTER FIVE

Emily stepped back.

"Waaaaaaaaaaah!" shrieked The Maggot as she stood on his tail. With her nerves already stretched to breaking point, Emily jumped violently and fell off the packing case. She might have hurt herself badly, but in the event she landed on a pile of cardboard boxes which broke her fall. The packing case, however, overturned and fell against a stack of metal oil containers which teetered, then tumbled with a noise like the end of the world.

"Who's that? What's going on out there?" Grandmother's voice called from deep inside the barn.

Emily scrambled to her feet. "Run for it Maggot!" She took to her heels in a cloud of terror. Her mother often read her fairy stories and she knew what happened when little girls were caught by the wicked witch.

Emily raced along the side of the barn. As she reached the front, the huge double doors opened and her grandmother stepped out, still wearing her pointed hat and carrying the broomstick. In her other hand, oddly enough, was what looked like a foil container from a Chinese take-away. It smelled of chop suey.

"Why, Emily, it's you," she said.

Emily ignored her and headed full tilt for the woods.

"Emily!" her grandmother called after her in surprise.

Emily disappeared into the trees. At least Grandmother couldn't fly her broomstick after her or she'd get knocked off by the branches. Emily plunged on and after a few moments left the track. She found a clump of bushes and crawled into the centre to hide.

"Emily!" Her grandmother's voice floated through the trees. "Emily, where are you?"

Emily shivered. It was bad enough that Farmer Osboro was a werewolf, but to find her grandmother was a witch was almost more than she could bear. How on earth did any little children manage to grow up in such a monstrously wicked world? But at least she was safe in the bushes. Grandmother would never find her here.

"Come out of those bushes at once!" her grandmother's voice commanded, so close that Emily jumped.

Emily crawled out sheepishly. The chances were she would be eaten or turned into a frog.

"You'll ruin your dress doing things like that," her grandmother said severely. "Then your mother will blame me." She reached out and took Emily's hand. "Come along to the cottage. You can wash your hands and knees and I'll make us a cup of tea. Is your mother with you?"

"No," mumbled Emily. She pushed out her bottom lip and looked about to cry.

"What's the matter, dear?" Grandmother asked at once.

"I don't want to be turned into a frog," said Emily. She didn't want to be eaten either, but it had occurred to her this was less likely since Grandmother was on a diet.

"Turned into a — ?" Grandmother exclaimed in amazement. She began, quite suddenly, to laugh. "Oh, you mean the —" She pointed to her black robe. "And the —" She pointed to her pointy hat. "And the —" Her laughter exploded in ripples that shook her plump body as she pointed to the broomstick.

"Yes," said Emily, taken aback.

"You thought I was a witch!" Grandmother roared delightedly.

"Aren't you?" asked Emily uncertainly.

"Of course I am!" her grandmother shrieked. "But witches don't waste time turning people into frogs! At least this one doesn't. Come back to the house and I'll tell you all about it."

In the living room of the cottage, Emily nursed a mug of tea and balanced a buttered scone on one recently-washed knee as her grandmother pushed another log onto the fire and began to talk.

"Witches aren't all bad," her grandmother said. "I know they're always bad in the fairy tales, but that's only because it makes the story more exciting. In real life, there are good witches and bad witches and to be honest, most of the witches I know are quite good."

"Only quite good?" Emily interrupted.

"Only quite good," her grandmother confirmed. "Like schoolteachers and bank managers and nurses and policemen and income tax inspectors. Most of them are quite good most of the time. Very few of them are very bad. People who are very bad are just as unusual as people who are very good — and you know how few people are very good." She sniffed, leaned back and took up her own mug of tea.

"Anyway, it doesn't matter about the rest of the witches in the world. The important thing is this witch. And whatever about the rest of the witches, I'm definitely a good witch. Not a very good witch, because that's as difficult as being a very good bank manager, but a good witch and perhaps even a better-than-average witch."

"So you don't turn people into frogs?" Emily asked.

"Wouldn't know how," her grandmother said.

"What do you do?"

"Well," said her grandmother slowly, "that's a little complicated. I make cures from plants and use them to heal people. And I cast spells to help people love one another. And I say prayers to stop people hurting the Earth —"

"Like the Green Party?" Emily interrupted again. She bit into the scone, which was delicious.

"Yes," her grandmother said solemnly.

"What else do you do?" Emily asked encouragingly. Now she'd found Grandmother wasn't a bad witch, she was fascinated.

"I try to help the crops grow and I like to see the cats round here are all as healthy as The Maggot and I encourage the birds to compose new and even more beautiful songs and I study the Ancient Wisdom and —"

Emily's ears pricked up at once. "What's the Ancient Wisdom, Grandmother?"

"In olden days, before even I was born, the people knew how to do a lot of things that they've forgotten now. Mysterious things, magical things. Some of this knowledge got written down in secret books and when you put them all together, those secret books add up to the Ancient Wisdom. I try to learn as much of it as I can."

"Would the Ancient Wisdom tell you what to do about a werewolf?" Emily asked.

"Oh, yes," her grandmother said easily. "First of all, you need to protect yourself by wearing a necklace made from a plant called wolfbane. Then you get a gun and you make a silver bullet which you load into the gun and you shoot the werewolf with the silver bullet. That's the only way to kill a werewolf. Nothing else works." She stopped. "What's the matter, dear?"

"I don't know where to get a gun, let alone a silver bullet," Emily said miserably. "And even if I did, I wouldn't know how to shoot one."

Frowning, her grandmother asked very quietly, "You haven't come across a werewolf, have you?"

Emily nodded. "Farmer Osboro," she said. "But I'm the only one who can see him change."

"That's not unusual," her grandmother said thoughtfully. "Werewolves have become very clever since the old days. That's why nobody believes in them any more. They still change into wolves, of course, but only very, very special people can actually see them do it."

"You mean I'm a very, very special person?" asked Emily in amazement.

"Yes, you are," said her grandmother, "although you may not be so pleased to hear this means you're the only one who can stop the werewolf. You, Emily. Nobody else can do it for you."

There was a grim silence in the room, broken only by the ticking of the grandfather clock. Distantly the cat-flap rattled and a moment later The Maggot strolled in with his tail high in the air.

He polished Emily's ankles, then jumped nimbly onto her grandmother's lap.

"I don't know how to stop a werewolf!" Emily wailed suddenly. "I don't have silver bullets or a gun or anything!" She sniffed. "They won't allow little girls to have guns."

"And quite right too," her grandmother muttered. "Give guns out to little girls and you'd never know who they would shoot. All the same —" She stared thoughtfully into the fire. "— I see your point. What you need is a different approach ..."

She stood up so abruptly that The Maggot had to leap from her lap. "You can read now, can't you dear?"

"Not very well," Emily admitted. "I still have trouble with the big words."

Her grandmother actually leaned into the fireplace and reached up the chimney. She emerged holding a small, soot-blackened book which she dusted off on her apron. She handed it to Emily.

"Never mind," she said, "this is mainly pictures anyway. But it will give you the idea if you study and practice hard." She sat down again and leaned forward eagerly. "You'll need a helper, of course, so I suggest you take The Maggot. He's what they used to call my familiar, so he's used to magic. I'm quite certain that between the two of you, you'll work out what to do about Farmer Osboro."

Emily looked at the little book. There were three words printed on the cover, but she only recognised the middle one, which was 'for'. She looked up at her grandmother. "What's the book called, Grandmother?"

"It's called Hypnosis for Beginners," her grandmother said.

# CHAPTER SIX

That evening after dinner, Emily went to her room early, pretending she was tired. She'd told her mother that she'd walked to Grandmother's and explained that The Maggot had walked back with her. She'd also explained that The Maggot had come to have a little holiday with them and that her grandmother had given permission. Emily's mother wasn't very sure about this, but since they were both going to see Grandmother the next day, she voiced no immediate objection.

Once in her room, Emily carefully closed the door, then propped her pillows so she could sit up in bed. She climbed in, crossed her legs, set her back against the pillows and opened the little book.

The first page had a picture of a pair of eyes and the same words that were printed on the cover. Since her grandmother had told her what these meant, she knew it said Hypnosis for Beginners. She turned the page.

There was a photograph on the next page of a tall man with deep set eyes and a small, pointed beard. He was wearing a formal suit and a top hat. His name, printed under the picture, was Prof Whammo. It seemed an odd sort of name to Emily, but she supposed he must be foreign. She turned another page.

There was a picture on this page as well. It showed Prof Whammo standing in front of a very pretty young woman in old-fashioned clothes, seated in a chair. Prof Whammo looked pleased with himself, which was very peculiar since the young woman was fast asleep. Emily knew it was rude to fall asleep when someone was talking to you, however boring they were, and could not understand why Prof Whammo wasn't annoyed at the young woman. She turned another page.

The heading on the page was:  HOW TO HYPNOTISE

Underneath the heading, Emily painfully read:

— Hypnosis is an art which almost anyone can learn *something* they are *something* to put in a great deal of *something*. The most *something something* in hypnosis is the use of your eyes. The *something* of your eyes is what *something* those who come in *something* with you and *something* you to bend them to your will. Thus, the first thing you must do to learn hypnosis is to *something* the *something* of your eyes. *Something something something* is —

It was useless. She just wasn't good enough at reading to be able to understand what this strange book was all about. She set it down on the bed as The Maggot jumped up beside her. "It's no good, Maggot," she told him. "I'm just not old enough for a grown-up book like that. And I can't ask Mummy to read it to me or she'll ask me where I got it and then I'd have to tell her Grandmother's secret."

"Wah," The Maggot said. He leaned over to stare short-sightedly at the book then reached out and flicked the page expertly with his paw. The next page had more pictures, drawings this time.

"Clever old Maggot," Emily said as she picked up the book again. You could tell a lot from pictures, sometimes more than you could from the words.

The first drawing showed a man with a little beard rather like Prof Whammo seated in a chair facing a young woman rather like the pretty young woman in the photograph, except that in the drawing she was wide awake. They were seated very close together so their knees were almost touching.

The next drawing was almost the same except that now Prof Whammo had raised one hand above his head. The young woman was staring at him intently.

The drawing after that was the most interesting of the three. It showed Prof Whammo leaning forward so that he was only about a foot from the young woman. Little lightning flashes were coming out of his eyes. The woman was gaping at him in astonishment.

In the final drawing on the page the woman had fallen forward, fast asleep, having apparently become bored with the little lightning flashes. There were words underneath each picture, but all far too long for Emily to read. She turned the page at once.

There were more drawings on the next page and they were astonishing drawings. They showed a smug Prof Whammo standing to one side while the young woman, still fast asleep, played an imaginary trombone, squatted on her chair like a hen on a perch and even turned a somersault so that her knickers showed.

Emily stared at the drawings in amazement. "So that's what it's all about!" she exclaimed to The Maggot. "When you hypnotise somebody, you can get them to do things." By the look of the drawings, you could get them to do just about anything you wanted.

She flicked through the remainder of the book. There were many more pictures, but they all showed much the same thing. When Prof Whammo made little lightning flashes come out of his eyes, people did what he told them, slept when he told them and woke up when he told them.

It was unbelievable. But it was exciting as well. Now she knew why her grandmother had given her the book. If she could somehow hypnotise Farmer Osboro, she could tell him not to throw Reggie McPhee over any more hedges. She could tell him not to be so bad-tempered in the future. She could tell him to be kind and gentle to all his animals instead of kicking them when they broke out of his field. Most important of all, she could tell him to stop changing into a werewolf. She wondered if she could make it work.

"This is very exciting, Maggot," she told The Maggot.

"Wah," The Maggot said excitedly.

She picked up the book again and went over every picture with enormous care. There was no doubt about it, the secret seemed to be in the little lightning flashes that came out of Prof Whammo's eyes.

At the far side of Emily's room was a dressing table and on the dressing table was a small hand mirror. She climbed down off the bed and retrieved it, showing The Maggot his reflection in the mirror as she climbed back up again. She held the glass about a foot from her face and stared intently. No lightning flashes came from her eyes.

"I'm not doing it right," she mumbled to The Maggot. She narrowed her eyes and tried again. Still no lightning flashes. She glanced back at the book. Maybe you had to sit in a particular way. But no, there were several different lightning flash drawings and Prof Whammo was in different positions in them all, sometimes sitting, sometimes standing, sometimes leaning forward, sometimes gesturing with his hand, sometimes not. Emily went back to the mirror.

This time she tried to imagine flashes coming out of her eyes. She had a very good imagination, clear and vivid, on account of daydreaming so much, so picturing the flashes wasn't very difficult. But somehow it didn't feel right. The drawings showed flashes coming out of Prof Whammo's eyes which meant something was going on, not just that somebody was imagining something was going on.

"I'll never do it," she muttered to The Maggot, who was sitting up, tail curled round his paws, watching her intently.

This time she took a deep breath and held it. She stared at herself in the mirror, watching her face grow red. Pressure began to build inside her head. She felt — and saw — her eyes begin to bulge.

After a moment her heart was thumping wildly and her chest felt as if it had caught fire, but she held on. At least something was happening, even though it was nothing like what was drawn in the book. The feeling of pressure suddenly became too much to bear and she released her breath explosively.

Just before she did so, little lightning flashes shot out of her eyes.

Emily sat panting, staring at her own reflection in the mirror. She was certain it had happened. Just a couple of tiny flashes half a second before she let out her breath. But if she could manage a couple of tiny flashes now, it meant that with practice she could manage more, maybe eventually manage a whole stream.

Fifteen minutes later, Emily could make lightning flashes to order and without having to hold her breath. The trick seemed to be to create a feeling of pressure inside your head and then direct all the pressure to the back of your eyes. If you managed to hold it there for a bit, your eyeballs started to feel itchy and after that the lightning flashes started. They weren't very bright or very big — in fact she doubted anyone who wasn't looking carefully would even notice them — but she could definitely see them in the mirror.

Would they make people fall asleep and do what they were told? Emily chewed her lip thoughtfully. She would have to try it out on somebody to make sure it worked before she'd dare to try it on Farmer Osboro. But who?

"Look into my eyes," said Emily firmly to The Maggot.

The Maggot leaned forward and peered intently into her eyes.

"Keep looking," Emily said. She concentrated on building the pressure inside her head.

When it was there, she directed it behind her eyes and waited, letting it build further.

"Wah," said The Maggot impatiently.

"Wait," Emily muttered, concentrating.

Abruptly the stream of little lightning flashes erupted from her eyes. The Maggot reacted as if pole-axed. His eyes widened momentarily, then closed. His fur stood on end.

His tail stiffened. He reared up convulsively, stretched full length, then fell flat on his back with all four feet in the air.

"Are you all right, Maggot?" Emily asked in sudden alarm.

"Wah," said The Maggot dreamily.

At least he wasn't dead. "Sit up, Maggot," Emily ordered tentatively. The Maggot rolled over and sat up at once.

"Jump down off the bed," said Emily, suppressing her excitement. The Maggot jumped gracefully down onto the floor.

It was time for something more complicated. Emily took a deep breath, her heart pounding. "Maggot," she ordered firmly, "stand on your hind legs and walk around the room!"

Without a second's hesitation, The Maggot stood up on his hind legs and set off round the room, eyes tight shut, his front paws stretched before him in the manner of a sleep-walker. He didn't even hesitate when Emily screamed excitedly, "I've done it! Whee! I've done it! Now just you wait, Farmer Osboro! Just you wait!"

# CHAPTER SEVEN

She was a lot less excited by the end of Monday afternoon.

After a weekend of practice with The Maggot under her belt, Emily felt confident of hypnotising anybody. She could make little lightning flashes stream out of her eyes with almost no effort now and had discovered she did not even have to face her subject. Even if she directed the flashes at the back of The Maggot's head, he fell over sideways. She'd also found he enjoyed being hypnotised. The minute he fell over, he would start to purr.

Monday started well enough. At break time while they were queuing for school milk, she cautiously sent some flashes into the unsuspecting skull of the boy in front of her, a dim but happy soul named Stephen Saltzman. To her relief, he did not fall over like The Maggot, but his shoulders slumped and his arms dangled at his sides like the arms of a rag doll.

"You will get my milk for me," Emily whispered. She didn't want to order him to do anything too odd in case it didn't work and she would have to explain what she was up to.

But she needn't have worried. "I will get your milk for you," echoed Stephen in a peculiar, hollow voice. He broke ranks, walked directly to the head of the queue, pushed somebody aside and grabbed a bottle of milk. He walked straight back to Emily. "Your milk, O Mighty One," he said in the same peculiar voice.

Somebody right at the back of the queue chanted, "Stevie's got a girl-friend!" But the rest held their peace. Stephen was a quiet boy, but enormous for his age. Emily blushed and took the milk. It had worked far better than she had expected. "Get back in place," she whispered, "and wake up."

"Yes, O Mighty One," Stephen said. He pushed back into the queue, shivered briefly, then shuffled forward with the rest as if nothing had happened.

Emily took her milk to the grassy bank behind the bicycle shed and sat down to drink and think. Stephen had been easy. But he was so dim he usually did what he was told anyway. The real test would be to try it on somebody difficult, somebody with a mind of their own, somebody who argued and walked off in a huff when they disagreed with you. Somebody like ...

"Hello, Wilhelmena," Emily said as Wilhelmena McPhee sat down beside her.

"Why did Stephen Saltzman get your milk?" asked Wilhelmena without preliminary.

"I don't know," Emily lied promptly. She'd long ago learned you should never tell a secret to Wilhelmena. It was like putting it on the BBC.

"Why did he call you 'O Mighty One'?" Wilhelmena insisted.

That was trickier. Claiming she didn't know again would never work. Emily said, "Stephen always calls people funny things. Hadn't you noticed?"

"No," said Wilhelmena flatly. "Specially not 'O Mighty One'.

He's never called me 'O Mighty One'. He's never called anybody

'O Mighty One'. What are you up to, Emily?"

Emily sent a stream of little lightning flashes into Wilhelmena's head. At once Wilhelmena's head fell forward and she began to snore lightly.

"You will forget all about Stephen Saltzman getting my milk," Emily ordered. "You will forget he ever called me 'O Mighty One'. And while you're at it, you'll mind your own business generally. Got that?"

"Yes, O Mighty One," said Wilhelmena.

"Now wake up," said Emily firmly.

Wilhelmena's eyes jerked open and she glanced around for a moment with a look of bewilderment on her face. But she only said, "Do you think it's going to rain?"

Emily looked up at the sky. "I don't think so."

"Good," said Wilhelmena. "I forgot to bring a coat today and I don't want to get my dress wet." She climbed to her feet and trotted off.

Emily finished her milk with a feeling of real satisfaction. If she could hypnotise Wilhelmena, she could hypnotise anybody — including Farmer Osboro. She thought she might even have a try today, right after school.

Fortunately she decided on one more test. Her victim this time was Peter Collins, a thin, frail, nervous creature with glasses. Emily had only ever known one living thing more timid than Peter and that was a hamster, so he should have been easy.

She found him sitting at the edge of the football field, his back against a tree, wincing each time there was body contact in the game.

"Hello, Peter," Emily said cheerfully.

"Hello, Emily," Peter said.

"Aren't you going to join in?" asked Emily, nodding towards the half dozen or so boys who were chasing a ball furiously around the field.

"Oh, no," Peter told her, eyes wide. "It's much too rough for me."

He glanced towards the game and Emily directed a stream of little lightning flashes into the side of his head. To her surprise he did not slump forward.

"Turn a somersault, Peter!" Emily commanded.

Peter looked at her with an expression of pure horror. "Oh, no, Emily. I might fall over and hurt myself."

Emily let him have it right between the eyes, flash after flash. "You will stand up and walk three times around the tree," she commanded.

"Why should I do that?" Peter asked.

"Because I told you to," said Emily. She kept her voice firm, but her confidence was draining away quickly.

"You're being very silly, Emily," Peter said. "Girls are often like that, I'm afraid. But I shall just ignore you." He sniffed, stood up and walked away, his head high.

Emily watched him go with a distinctly sinking feeling.

She'd given him her best shot and nothing had happened. Why? It couldn't be because he was a boy. Stephen Saltzman was a boy. It couldn't be because he was clever. Wilhelmena McPhee was just as clever and she'd fallen asleep very satisfactorily.

It was obvious she needed to try a few more experiments. But before she could do so, the bell rang for class. That put paid to any more hypnosis for a while and Emily's frustration had reached screaming pitch when Mrs Wilson was called away to take a phone call.

In the general uproar that followed, Emily crept up on Reggie McPhee, apparently none the worse for his descent into the rose-bed. She unleashed the lightning flashes into his right ear and watched with relief as his head slumped. "When Mrs Wilson comes back, you will need to go to the lavatory," she whispered. "Now wake up quickly."

Reggie's head jerked up and he looked around him with an expression of bewilderment. Emily went back to her desk.

The class fell reluctantly silent as Mrs Wilson returned. "Now —" she began.

Reggie McPhee stood up. "Please, Mrs Wilson, may I leave the room?" He looked sort of desperate.

"Don't be long, Reggie," Mrs Wilson said kindly and smiled a little as he streaked from the classroom.

Emily should have felt relieved, but the mystery was as deep as ever. If Wilhelmena and Reggie and Stephen all did what they were told, why hadn't it worked on Peter?

When the bell sounded for swimming class, Emily went to get her coat from the cloakroom and quietly zapped a girl called Freda Williams who came to school each day with a different bow in her hair. She made Freda pretend to be a ballet dancer with no problem at all. Like most of the others, Freda murmured, "Yes, O Mighty One" to acknowledge the command.

Emily was beginning to feel relieved. So far, Peter was the only one who had given any trouble and she began to wonder if it had been something as simple as the way she aimed the flashes. Then, standing in the queue for the bus to the swimming baths, she tried twice more — an older girl whose name she didn't know and a boy named Craig Thompson. Neither showed the slightest reaction to the lightning flashes and when she tried to order them to do things, they looked at her in something like amazement.

She had two more goes on the bus itself. One was a resounding success. A boy called Joe Strummer changed seats seven times on her order to the irritation of everybody else in the vehicle. But a girl named Valerie Rankin just stared out the window and ignored her when the lightning flashes struck.

At the end of the school day Emily walked through her mother's grocery shop into the flat behind in a state of heavy depression. It seemed that some people could be hypnotised and some could not and the only way to find out which was which was to try it and see. This left her very nervous.

She could imagine what might happen if she tried to hypnotise Farmer Osboro and failed. All the same, she knew she had to do something ... and soon.  If she didn't, Farmer Osboro might well attack another child or kick another sheep.

# CHAPTER EIGHT

Emily's mother was looking even more gloomy than usual. Over a dinner of lamb chops, Emily discovered the reason. Somebody had told her mother in the morning that the new Magnum Supermarket was going to open on the twelfth of July and it had ruined her entire day. Emily listened to the bad news as sympathetically as she could, but her mind wasn't on it. All she could think about was Farmer Osboro and what she had to do.

The trouble was, she didn't know exactly what to do, so as quickly as she could decently manage after dinner she excused herself and went up to her room. The Maggot was sprawled on her bed.

"Hello, Maggot," Emily said absently. "What am I going to do about Farmer Osboro changing into a werewolf?"

The Maggot sat up and glanced around him nervously.

Emily sat on the edge of the bed, her feet dangling. "The thing is," she told The Maggot, "Farmer Osboro seems to change every time something annoys him. I have to do something right away."

"Wah," said The Maggot sympathetically.

"The trouble is," said Emily, "I don't know what to do."

The Maggot jumped off her bed and walked over to the pile of

cushions under which she'd hidden Hypnosis for Beginners. He began to scratch at the pile.

"Well, yes..." said Emily uncertainly. "I thought that too. I mean, when Grandmother gave me the book and I managed to make the little lightning flashes come out of my eyes, I thought that's what I'd do. But Grandmother never mentioned the flashes don't work on everybody. So what happens if I try to hypnotise Farmer Osboro and it doesn't work on him?"

"Wah," said The Maggot, shaking his head slowly.

"No," said Emily thoughtfully, "I don't know either. But that's not the worst of it. Can you imagine what would happen if he actually changed into a werewolf while I was trying to hypnotise him?"

The Maggot fell over on his back and allowed his tongue to loll out of his mouth.

"Exactly!" Emily said as he climbed back on his feet again. "He'd kill me and eat me alive." She stared into the middle distance. "But I think I'm going to have to risk it, Maggot. There doesn't seem to be anything else to do."

"Wah," said The Maggot encouragingly. He jumped back on the bed and polished her elbow with his broad, furry head.

The next morning Emily arrived in school in such a state of nerves that she had to sit on her hands to keep them from shaking. But by the time the bell rang for class, she had sunk into a state of icy calm. Although Mrs Wilson had not yet appeared, Emily sat down at her desk at once. While all around her the class was talking, shouting and chasing round the room, she carefully took out her wooden ruler and her new exercise book with the feint blue lines.

As Reggie McPhee pulled Madelene O'Mara's hair and Stephen Saltzman ran off with Little Willie Craig's cap, Emily tore a sheet of paper from her exercise book. Using her best and clearest handwriting, she pencilled: **MEET ME IN THE PLAYGROUND.** *Emily*

Then she folded the paper in half along its length, opened it out again and folded the two top corners in to meet the centre fold. This left her with a pointed page. She folded back from the point towards the middle, then re-folded along the centre crease.

"Good morning, class!" said Mrs Wilson as she bustled through the door. "Settle down, please."

The uproar gradually eased as children took their seats. Emily folded wings to make a paper dart.

"This morning," Mrs Wilson said cheerfully, "I want you to practise your transcription." There was a general groan from the class. Transcription meant copying passages from a text book into your note pad and was probably the most boring occupation in the history of humanity. Mrs Wilson ignored them. She opened the large cupboard beside her desk and took out a pile of green text books. "I want you to transcribe from these."

As Mrs Wilson turned away, Emily launched her dart in the direction of Stephen Saltzman. It sailed in a beautiful arc and landed in his messy hair. Stephen slapped at it wildly like someone attacked

by an insect, then discovered what it was and pulled it out to look at it more closely. For one awful moment Emily thought he might crumple it up, or, worse still, throw it at someone else. But what he did was unfold it.

"Will you give these out, Sarah-Sue?" Mrs Wilson asked a girl in the front row.

Stephen Saltzman read the note and looked across wide-eyed at Emily. Emily at once put up her hand.

"Yes, Emily?" Mrs Wilson asked.

"Please, Mrs Wilson, may I be excused to leave the room?"

"Couldn't you have gone before we started class?" Mrs Wilson asked severely.

"I'm sorry, Mrs Wilson," Emily said. She waited.

"Oh, go on with you - but don't be long!"

"Thank you, Mrs Wilson." Emily stood up. As she did so, Stephen Saltzman's hand shot up.

"Please, Mrs Wilson," Stephen Saltzman said, "may I be excused to leave the room? I have to go to the toilet too, Mrs Wilson, ever so urgent. May I, Mrs Wilson, may I?"

Emily walked out and closed the classroom door. Instead of making for the girl's cloakroom, she walked quickly down the corridor and out of the school building. She waited in the playground just outside the door.

Stephen Saltzman joined her almost at once. "I got your note," he said. "When I told Mrs Wilson I wanted to go to the toilet too she said was it something catching." He giggled. "Do you want to kiss me?"

Emily hit him with a stream of lightning flashes right between the eyes. When Stephen's eyes glazed over, she said firmly, "You will go back to Mrs Wilson and tell her I was feeling ill." It was no less than the truth. Her legs were jelly, her knees were knocking and her stomach was lying on its back with its feet in the air.

"I will go back to Mrs Wilson and tell her you were feeling ill, O Mighty One," Stephen Saltzman echoed.

"You will tell her I couldn't come back to class." This was true as well. What she had to do was far more important than any transcription. "You will tell her I will be in tomorrow." If, Emily thought, she survived Farmer Osboro.

"I will do as you command, O Mighty One," said Stephen Saltzman. He turned and walked woodenly back into the school.

Emily worried vaguely somebody might notice he was hypnotised before the trance wore off, but decided the risk was small. Stephen was a bit odd at the best of times. She closed her eyes and sighed, then said a short prayer for help in what she had to do.

In minutes she had left the playground and was walking, heart pounding, down the village street. The lane leading to the Osboro farm was no more than five minutes away, at the opposite end of the village from her grandmother's cottage.

She felt more nervous than ever as she approached the grey stone farmhouse. Suppose Farmer Osboro wasn't home? Suppose there was somebody with him? Suppose he couldn't be hypnotised? She entered the farmyard, glancing nervously towards the cowshed. There was no sign of Farmer Osboro outside. She went across to the house, where a pair of wellington boots stood by the back door, but Farmer Osboro wasn't in them. She stopped at the door and looked up at the heavy iron knocker, wondering if she would ever find the courage to use it.

She might have stood there for the rest of the day listening to her heart pounding, but the door swung open suddenly and Farmer Osboro was looking down at her. He hadn't changed into a werewolf (at least not yet) but he was a terrifying sight all the same.

"Yes?" he demanded.

Emily stared up at him, too frightened to say anything.

Farmer Osboro scowled. "Did you want to see me, little girl?"

Emily's terror broke abruptly. "Yes, Farmer Osboro," she said. Then, hoping against hope he would hypnotise as easily as Stephen Saltzman, she unleashed a stream of little lightning flashes to zap him right between the eyes.

# CHAPTER NINE

"If you do want to see me, you'd better hurry up and tell me what it's all —" Farmer Osboro was saying. He stopped. His eyes widened and began to spin. His mouth opened then closed and his teeth began to dance and chatter. A whirring noise started. It seemed to be coming from his ears as if his brains were working far too fast.  He howled.

Startled, Emily switched off the stream of little lightning flashes, but it made no difference. Farmer Osboro raised both arms above his head, curled his hands into fists and brought them both crashing down on the surface of the door.

"Digga digga digga!" chattered Farmer Osboro. Slowly, but with increasing speed, he began to spin on his own axis like a demented ballet dancer. "Wheee!" he screamed.

Blurring like a top, he spun into his own farmyard, now moving so fast that little tendrils of smoke crawled out of his socks as friction produced heat. Emily stepped back in alarm. Nothing like this had ever happened before when she tried to hypnotise someone. But then again, she'd never tried to hypnotise a werewolf before.

The spinning Farmer Osboro collided with the wall of a cowshed, which cracked alarmingly and threw off a large, flat lump of plaster.

"Waaaaaah!" he wailed and slowed to a stop. He jerked forward to touch his toes, snapped upright again, then repeated the whole process over and over, jerking and snapping like a clockwork toy.

"Dinga-ding-ding!" sang Farmer Osboro. He began to dance, throwing arms and legs in opposite directions. He danced around the farmyard, then climbed up to dance upon a huge round bale of straw. "Dinga," he sang. "Dinga-ding-ding!" He danced too near the edge and disappeared suddenly with a crash that shook his house.

"Farmer Osboro ...?" Emily whispered uncertainly.

Farmer Osboro shot upright like a rocket taking off from Cape Canaveral. His clothes were rumpled and, in places, torn. His hair looked like someone had plugged his nose into an electric socket. His eyes had developed little spirals which spun and spun, surrounded by dancing stars. "Tweet!" he went. "Tweet-tweet, tweet-tweet!" He snapped to attention. "Your wish is my command, O Mighty One," he said.

He was hypnotised! Emily felt a surge of relief so strong she had to steady herself against the door. All the same, she thought she'd better check to make absolutely sure. The thing was to order him to do something that wouldn't send him into a fury if he wasn't hypnotised. She took a deep breath.

"Would you please pick up your wellington boots, Farmer Osboro?" she asked politely.

"Yes, O Mighty One," he said. He picked up the boots.

Emily watched him cautiously. He certainly seemed to be hypnotised all right. The 'O Mighty One' business was a bit of a giveaway. But now, just for the sake of safety, she needed to test him properly. "Put one boot on top of your head!" she ordered bravely.

The farmer balanced a boot on top of his head and stood stiffly to attention.

"Now dance a little jig," said Emily.

"Deedly-eye-die-die," sang Farmer Osboro as he broke into an Irish jig. "Deedle eadle eadle eadle." He looked a complete wally.

"Stop," said Emily as the boot fell off his head. She felt confident now. "Listen carefully," she said, "because I am going to give you some very important orders."

"Yes, O Mighty One." Farmer Osboro stopped jigging and stood to attention. He had an expression of almost idiotic interest on his face.

Emily fixed him with her most powerful stare, even going so far as to unleash a couple of small lightning flashes to emphasise her words. "From now on," she said very slowly and carefully, "you will never ever change into a werewolf again. Do you understand?"

"I understand, O Mighty One," said Farmer Osboro blankly. "I will never ever change into a werewolf again."

"Not ever," Emily said forcefully.

"Not ever," the farmer echoed.

That seemed to be that. But there were one or two additional points Emily wanted cleared up, just in case. "As well as never ever changing into a werewolf again, you will never ever lose your temper with any child again," she said.

"I will never ever lose my temper with any child again, O Mighty One," said Farmer Osboro hollowly.

"Or ever throw anyone over a hedge."

"Or ever throw anyone over a hedge, O Mighty One," said Farmer Osboro.

"Or kick a sheep or any other animal," Emily added.

"I shall never again do that, O Mighty One," Farmer Osboro assured her.

Was there anything else? Something was nibbling like a mouse at the edge of her memory. Suddenly she remembered. "You will forget I was ever here."

"I have forgotten already, O Mighty One."

"That's good," said Emily with considerable satisfaction. "You will wake up as soon as I have gone." Without waiting for an answer, she turned to go. As she did so, she heard behind her a blood-curdling growl.

Emily froze for a moment, then turned. Farmer Osboro was no longer at attention in his farmyard, but crouched on top of the round bale of straw. His face was covered in fur, thin lips rolled back to reveal long, glistening fangs and a furry tail stretched out behind him. Despite everything she'd ordered, he was a werewolf again!

"You weren't supposed to do that!" Emily shouted in alarm.

"I didn't," said the thing crouched on the bale. "You only told the farmer not to turn into a werewolf. I'm the werewolf that turns into a farmer!"

It didn't make a lot of sense, but Emily realised she had no time to think about it. She let rip another stream of lightning flashes.

The werewolf grinned. "No use trying that, my girl. Werewolves are immune. The only thing that stops me is a silver bullet and unless I'm very much mistaken, you don't have too many of those about your person." He leaped from the bale and rushed towards her like an express train.

Emily ran.

She ran down the lane and onto the village street. There was no-one to help. Everybody in the entire village seemed to be inside at that precise moment. Not that they would have been able to see the werewolf anyway. Emily streaked down the street and around the corner. The thing behind her howled and hurled itself in hot pursuit.

The street seemed to stretch out endlessly before her. She was a sturdy girl who could run quite fast, but all the same she felt the werewolf gain on her. The creature moved at incredible speed, although it slowed a little every time it howled. All the same, by the time she reached the entrance to the school playground, she thought she could feel its breath on the back of her neck. Fear gave her an extra burst of speed. The playground was surrounded by a high wire fence with only two exits. One led onto the street, the other opened into a lane which led to the playing fields. Emily ran through the second one without a moment's thought. She glanced behind her as she did so and saw the werewolf was no more than fifty yards away and gaining fast.

Emily ran up the lane, heart pounding, but already she knew she had made a dreadful mistake. Once she reached the playing field, there was nowhere else to go. Like the playground, the playing field was fenced and apart from the entrance by the lane, the only other way out was kept locked by Mr Morrow, who taught gym and games. She was running full tilt into a trap. Once the lane finished, the wolf had her cornered.

Since there was nothing else to do, Emily continued to run. But fast as her feet were travelling, her head was travelling faster. Terror made her mind work at top speed. Silver bullet, she thought. Where could she get a silver bullet? She couldn't, but did that really mean there was no way she could zap the werewolf?

She reached the playing field entrance and discovered a new horror. This gate was locked too. Mr Morrow must have closed that one as well. She turned. The werewolf was racing up the path, flecks of foam flying from its muzzle. There was nowhere for her to run, nowhere for her to hide. It would be on her in seconds.

What to do? What to do? The werewolf said it could only be stopped by a silver bullet, but she didn't think werewolves were above telling lies. But her grandmother had said the same and her grandmother —

Her grandmother, Emily thought. When she'd looked through the window of the barn, her grandmother had been casting a spell!

She'd been stirring a pot and chanting. And Emily had heard the words!

If Emily chanted the spell, would it work against the wolf? She didn't know what the spell was all about, hadn't thought to ask Grandmother. It might be a spell to make the crops grow, which wouldn't do much good. Or it might be a love spell, in which case the werewolf might fall in love with her, which at least would stop him eating her. Or it might be —

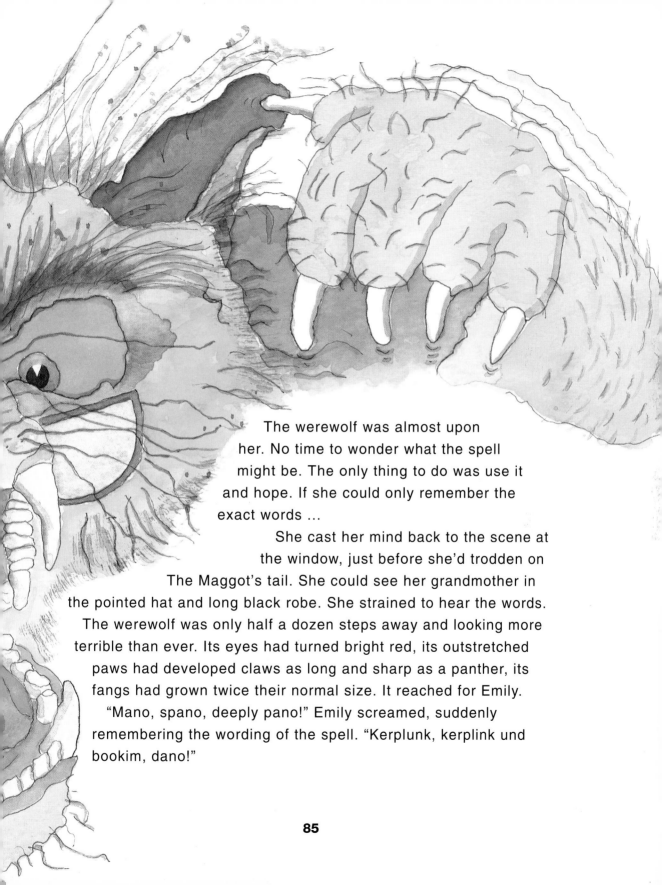

The werewolf was almost upon her. No time to wonder what the spell might be. The only thing to do was use it and hope. If she could only remember the exact words …

She cast her mind back to the scene at the window, just before she'd trodden on The Maggot's tail. She could see her grandmother in the pointed hat and long black robe. She strained to hear the words. The werewolf was only half a dozen steps away and looking more terrible than ever. Its eyes had turned bright red, its outstretched paws had developed claws as long and sharp as a panther, its fangs had grown twice their normal size. It reached for Emily.

"Mano, spano, deeply pano!" Emily screamed, suddenly remembering the wording of the spell. "Kerplunk, kerplink und bookim, dano!"

There was a silent explosion and the werewolf turned into a
barbecued spare rib.

# CHAPTER TEN

The spare rib smelled good, as Chinese food usually did, and relief made Emily feel extremely hungry. But since her mother had always told her never to eat anything that had fallen on the ground, she resisted the urge. Instead she wrapped the rib carefully in a tissue she was carrying and dropped it in the pocket of her dress. She felt relieved and excited all at once. What would have happened if the spell hadn't worked? How could she have stopped a savage werewolf? It was all too dreadful to think about.

Distantly she heard the school bell sounding for the end of class and the end of her school day. It was a bit of a blessing, since she didn't fancy facing Mrs Wilson just yet. She set off down the lane a lot more cheerfully than she had run up it.

"Have a good day at school, dear?" asked her mother as she walked into the shop. Her mother looked pale as well as tired and Emily hoped she wasn't going down with anything.

"Yes, thank you, Mother," she said politely.

"Do anything interesting?" her mother asked.

"Just used my exercise book," Emily said, thinking of the dart she'd shot at Stephen Saltzman.

"That's nice, dear," her mother said absently.

"Did you have a nice day, Mother?" Emily asked. She always liked to inquire.

Her mother sighed. "I'm afraid the stories are all true, Emily. Magnum Supermarkets are opening on the twelfth of next month."

"Are you quite sure?" Emily asked. "People often get things wrong."

"Quite sure," her mother said. "Look at this." She pulled a square of paper from her pocket and unfolded it. "Grand Opening, July 12th," she read. "Thousands of bargains." She looked at Emily. "Our customers won't stay with us when there are thousands of bargains just up the road. They're selling baked beans at a price I can't even manage to buy them for."

"Perhaps it's a very small tin," Emily suggested.

"Perhaps it is," her mother said tiredly.

Later that afternoon, Emily went out to play hopscotch with her friend Angela Wilkins. On her third turn, as she was making a particularly violent hop, the wrapped rib fell from her pocket. The Maggot, who was watching the game, shot forward like a ferret and grabbed the package.

"Maggot!" Emily shouted in sudden alarm. But he was off and running, ripping the tissue as he did so. She watched with horror as he shot up a nearby tree, then crouched in a fork where he proceeded to eat the spare rib with enormous gusto.

Emily dragged herself into school next morning with a feeling of dread hanging over her like a smoky cloud. She'd hardly slept at all the night before, worrying about what had happened. She didn't really understand what was going on, but could not shake off a horrifying suspicion that The Maggot had in some way eaten Farmer Osboro. And while she certainly had not approved of Farmer Osboro's werewolf habits, she did not think he deserved to be eaten for them. It was all very depressing.

She entered the playground and almost fell down in a faint. Farmer Osboro, with no bits eaten off him, was striding through the door marked BOYS. She stared after him, blinking to make sure her eyes were working right. She had never seen Farmer Osboro anywhere near her school before. What was he doing here today? Maybe it didn't have anything to do with her hypnotising him the day before, but she wouldn't care to bet on it. Maybe Farmer Osboro remembered, despite what she'd said to him. Maybe he remembered and had come to school to get his own back.

Trying to make sense of it all wasn't easy.

She'd hypnotised the farmer and forbidden him to change into a werewolf. Then a werewolf had appeared which claimed it liked to change into a farmer. Then she'd changed the werewolf into a spare rib. Then The Maggot changed the spare rib into cat food. And now, just one day later, she was back at school and by the looks of it, Farmer Osboro was here to get her. It was all very confusing, not to mention terrifying.

With nothing else to do she went into class.

"Hello, Emily," Mrs Wilson said. "Are you feeling better?"

"Yes, thank you, Mrs Wilson," said Emily without conviction.

"Was it something you ate?"

"I think it had to do with a barbecued spare rib, Mrs Wilson," Emily said truthfully.

Mrs Wilson smiled. "Well, at least you're back now. Which is just as well because I understand Farmer Osboro has called to see you. I don't know what it's about but he's in the Headmaster's study. You'd best not keep him waiting."

Emily knocked on the Headmaster's study door in a distinctly nervous state, well prepared to unleash her lightning flashes a second time. But Mr Simpson, the Headmaster, seemed perfectly friendly as he opened the door.

"Ah, Emily," he beamed, "I have Farmer Osboro to see you. I gather he has something to say to you privately, so I'll leave you two alone."

"Oh, no, Headmas —" Emily began to protest. But it was too late. Mr Simpson pushed her inside the study and closed the door behind him as he strode off down the corridor.

Emily turned warily. Farmer Osboro was standing by the Headmaster's desk. He looked exactly as he had done yesterday, very large, very red, very threatening.

Then his purple face broke into a beaming grin.

"Emily!" he gushed. "My dear, dear Emily! I wanted to thank you personally for freeing me from that dreadful werewolf thing. You have no idea what a relief it is not to have to worry about turning into that creature any more. Thank you. Thank you. Thank you." And to Emily's horror he actually bent down and kissed her.

"Don't mention it," said Emily, surreptitiously wiping away the kiss with the back of her hand.

"If there is anything," said Farmer Osboro, "anything at all I can do to repay your kindness, you have only to ask." He smiled at her. "Is there anything I can do?"

"No thank you, Farmer Osboro," Emily said. She still felt highly uncomfortable. The only thing she really wanted was to get away from this man and forget the whole sorry affair. Dealing with werewolves was really not a job for a little girl.

"Isn't there anything? Any little thing you want? Any small trouble you need help on? Any problem that's been worrying you?"

"Only my mother," Emily said, "and there's nothing much you can do about that."

"What's the matter with your mother?" Farmer Osboro asked. "Is she ill?"

"Not really," Emily said. "She's just frightened by the new supermarket that's supposed to open up the road from us next month. My mother runs a grocer's shop, you see and the new supermarket will take all her customers away."

"You're not talking about the new Magnum Supermarket by any chance?" asked Farmer Osboro.

Emily nodded. "Yes, sir."

To her astonishment, Farmer Osboro did an excited little dance, a shade more graceful than the one he'd done the day before. "But that's no problem at all!" he exclaimed. "My brother owns the Magnum Supermarket chain. I'll get him to put his supermarket somewhere else."

Emily's heart leaped. "Would you? Would you really?"

"I'll certainly try!" said Farmer Osboro expansively, reaching for the phone on the Headmaster's desk. "It's the very least I can do for the girl who saved me from the werewolf."

A sudden doubt struck her. "But suppose your brother won't agree to put it somewhere else, Farmer Osboro? Suppose it's too late to put it anywhere else. What will you do then?"

Farmer Osboro frowned, his hand poised over the phone. "I suppose I could always ask him to make your mother manageress of the new branch. That way she'd earn a lot of money for far less work than she's doing now."

It sounded like a dream come true for Emily. All the same, she hesitated.

"But suppose he won't make her manageress?" she protested.

"In that case," said Farmer Osboro seriously, "I'd just have to let you hypnotise him." And he treated Emily to a most enormous wink.

First published 1993 in UK by **Liber Press Ltd.**,
Kirklea Farm, Badgworth, Axbridge, Somerset, BS26 2QH

Text copyright © **J. H. Brennan** 1993
Illustrations copyright © **David Pace** 1993
All rights reserved.

A CIP catalogue record for this book is available from the British Library.
ISBN  1-85734-028-0

Printed and bound in Hong Kong
by WING KING TONG Co. Ltd.